BBC Children's Books
Published by the Penguin Group
Penguin Books Ltd, 80 Strand, London, WC2R 0RL, England
Penguin Group (USA) Inc., 375 Hudson Street, New York 10014, USA
Penguin Books (Australia) Ltd, 250 Camberwell Road, Camberwell,
Victoria 3124, Australia
(A division of Pearson Australia Group PTY Ltd)
Penguin Group (NZ), 67 Apollo Drive, Rosedale, Auckland
0632, New Zealand (a division of Pearson New Zealand Ltd)
Canada, India, South Africa
Published by BBC Children's Books, 2012
Text and design © Children's Character Books
Written and edited by Jason Loborik
Designed by Jason McEvoy
Pages 12-17 and 36-41 drawn by John Ross, colours by James Offredi
Pages 26-27 illustrated by Lee Sullivan
001 - 10 9 8 7 6 5 4 3 2 1

ISBN: 9781405908443
Printed in China

What's inside...

BACK INTO THE SHADOWS...

He's travelled through time and space for hundreds of years, battling monsters and righting wrongs. But while the Doctor continues to discover the wonders of the universe, could his past finally be catching up with him?

According to his old friend, Dorium Maldovar, the Doctor has had a long and dangerous life, but it's his future that the Silence believe to be infinitely more terrifying. They have foreseen a time when the oldest question in the universe will be asked – Doctor who? – a question they believe must never, ever be answered. And it's a question the Doctor has seemingly been running from all of his life...

The Silence's fear of the future not only spells great danger for the Doctor, but also has terrible consequences for his ever-faithful companions, Amy and Rory. Their precious baby daughter, Melody Pond – the child of the TARDIS – has been kidnapped by the Silence and raised with just one purpose in life – to destroy the Doctor!

However, all doesn't go quite according to plan. An older Melody escapes the Silence's clutches, and when she at last encounters the Doctor, she regenerates into a woman he's already met – the gun-toting, time-travelling archaeologist River Song – whose

wild adventures with the Doctor never seem to happen in the right order. Despite their apparent knowledge of the future, the Silence haven't foreseen that River Song would end up falling in love with the Doctor, or that she would even be willing to sacrifice her remaining lives to save his.

Some time later, the Silence try again and imprison River Song in an armed and automated spacesuit. But even though River knows the Doctor's death is a fixed point in time, she cannot bring herself to pull the trigger. Instead she would rather condemn the universe and see all of time and space fall apart...

Ultimately, the Doctor must sacrifice his own life to restore order and allow time to take its correct course. Or so it would appear. In reality, he manages to cheat death by cheating time itself, and at the appointed hour he takes refuge inside an android duplicate of himself, surviving the deadly blasts of energy.

With the events at Lake Silencio behind him, the Doctor believes he has finally learned his lesson. To some he had become an undefeatable hero, to others a dark and mysterious legend – while many had even considered him a god. He decides it's better that the universe believes he's dead at last. Time he stepped back into the shadows...

WHERE'S THE DOCTOR?

The Doctor's gone missing, but where could he be?
On the following pages, you'll discover various picture clues revealing a different letter. Simply re-arrange all the letters at the end, to find out the Doctor's mysterious location!

Q What is the Doctor's time-ship called? Write down the 3rd letter of its name in this space.

SERVANTS OF THE
SILENCE!

They call themselves the Sentinels of History, and believe the Doctor must be killed before the oldest question in the universe can be answered...

The Silents

These creepy-looking aliens are memory-proof, which means that as soon as you look away from them you forget they even existed. They can fire lethal bolts of energy from their long fingers, reducing human flesh to charred fragments in just a few seconds.

The Headless Monks

These fearsome fighters believe in following their hearts, not their minds – and so they deliberately chop their own heads off! A bit like the alien Silents, they shoot blasts of energy from their hands and can even electrify their swords to make them even more deadly.

Madame Kovarian

This sinister woman helped kidnap the real Amy and watched over her until she gave birth to baby Melody. She also organised the kidnapping of River Song, forcing her to lie in wait under Lake Silencio until it was time for her to kill the Doctor!

Colonel Manton

On Demons Run, the Doctor managed to trick Manton's soldiers into disarming themselves, before taking control of the Colonel's entire base. The Doctor told the Colonel to order his men to run away, hoping that Manton would forever be known as 'Colonel Runaway'!

Father Gideon Vandaleur

Gideon was an envoy of the Silence. Some time after he died, the shape-changing Teselecta took on his identity – the cover it needed to investigate the Silence in secret.

Gantok

The Doctor got Gantok to take him to the Seventh Transept, where he hoped the head of Dorium Maldovar would tell him more about the Silence. Gantok was about to shoot the Doctor for beating him at Live Chess, but then he fell into a pit of flesh-eating skulls and was killed himself!

MELS' DIARY

Even before she became known as River Song, young Melody loved to keep a secret diary...

Wednesday 10th April

Amelia went crazy at school today. She threw water all over Dozy Dylan cos he didn't believe her story about the Raggedy Doctor and kept saying she had a screw loose. I told her not to keep going on about the Doctor every five minutes. Nobody except for me is ever going to believe she knows a funny man in a time machine shaped like a phone box.

Thursday 11th April

Went to Amelia's house after school to play. Rory was waiting for us - as usual. I don't think he's got any other friends. Amelia wanted to play skipping games all night and Rory fell over 17 times. He still didn't want to go home though. Helped Amelia make yet another model of the Doctor out of toilet rolls.

Friday 12th April

Got sent to Mr Markham AGAIN for making Miss Wolsey shout. She turned purple this time - so funny! Amelia said I shouldn't have called Miss Wolsey stupid for not knowing why the Great Fire of London started. I tried to explain that it began after a big fight between the Doctor and some aliens, but she didn't want to listen. It's not my fault if she doesn't know even the FIRST THING about history!

Friday 5th June

Amy took the mick out of Rory's Roman fancy dress ALL NIGHT at Sasha's birthday party. Anyone can tell she SOOOOO fancies him.

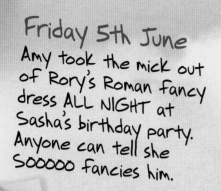

Saturday 6th June

Maddest day EVER!!! Missed the last bus home and got stranded at Gloucester bus station. Had no money for a taxi, so decided to have a go at driving the bus myself. Looked easy enough, but the steering must have been dodgy cos I swerved off the road and drove through the railings of the botanical gardens. Tried to point out to the police that no one was hurt, but they didn't see the funny side. Amy went mental AGAIN when she came to meet me. Anyone would think she was my mum or something. Ha-ha!

Sunday 7th June

Got REALLY fed up with both of them today. Rory's spent just about every day round Amy's house for the last 18 years, and she still can't spot the blindingly obvious. Decided to help out and do a bit of match-making. Probably broken some Law of Time or other, but who cares?! Bit weird though, getting my parents together and creating my own future. Must remember to ask the Doctor about it when I get to meet him...

THE DOCTOR

THE ZENTRABOT INVASION

NOW *QUIET*, ABBY, DON'T MAKE A SOUND!

CrEEEAAAK!

OOPS, SORRY!

WHAT DID I *JUST SAY?*

I DON'T THINK THEY HEARD!

SEE ANYTHING, DANNY?

YOU BET. LET'S *GO FOR IT!*

HEY, LOOK WHAT *I* GOT!

WOO-HOO, A NEW BOARD. *BEST CHRISTMAS EVER!*

DO YOU THINK IT'S A *ZENTRABOT?*

ONLY *ONE WAY* TO FIND OUT...

NO!!!

DANNY, ABBY, DON'T EVEN *THINK* ABOUT OPENING THAT PRESENT. IF YOU DO, IT'LL BE THE END OF YOU *BOTH!*

WHO ARE YOU? WHAT ARE YOU *DOING IN OUR HOUSE?*

AND HOW DO YOU KNOW OUR *NAMES?*

OH, THAT'S EASY. BEFORE I GOT HERE, I ACCIDENTALLY LANDED *THIRTY YEARS* IN THE FUTURE. DANNY, YOUR KIDS LOOK *JUST* LIKE YOU. *SAME NOSE* AND EVERYTHING.

BUT IF THIS TIMELINE GETS *RE-WRITTEN*, THEN IT'S BYE-BYE TO YOUR *TWINS!*

ARE YOU *FOR REAL?*

MUM! DAD! THERE'S A *NUTTER* IN THE HOUSE!

NO, THERE ISN'T, ABBY, THERE'S A *DOCTOR* IN THE HOUSE. OH, AND *MERRY CHRISTMAS.*

AHA! MORE *MAGNON EMISSIONS.* I KNEW IT!

WHIRRRRRRR!

RRRIPPP!

THE ACTIVATION SIGNAL'S *BREAKING THROUGH.* I CAN TRACE ITS *SOURCE...*

BZZZZZ!

...BUT I CAN'T *JAM IT...*

BEEEEP!

RUN!

OUCH! I'M GETTING REALLY *FED UP* WITH EVERYONE DOING THAT!

YOU TWO, *GET OUT OF HERE!*

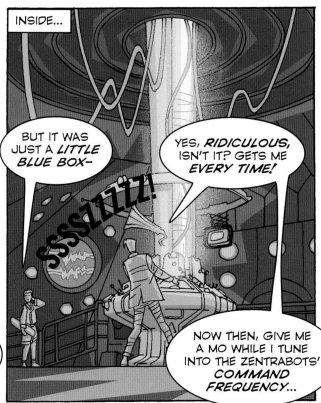

SIMPLE. I'VE PROGRAMMED IT TO *REPROGRAM* THE NEXT ZENTRABOT IT MEETS. THEN THAT ZENTRABOT WILL REPROGRAM THE NEXT AND...

ER, DOCTOR...

CAPTAIN KARVOX WISHES TO SEE YOU. *MOVE!*

OOPS!

SOON...

BY THE GODS, *WHAT AN INSULT!* IS THIS PATHETIC PAIR OF *VEEZEL-SNAPES* REALLY THE BEST EARTH CAN SEND AGAINST ME?

I'M WARNING YOU, CAPTAIN. *RETURN YOUR HOSTAGES*, OR I'LL GIVE THE *SIGNAL* FOR THE *ZENTRABOTS* TO ATTACK YOUR GUARDS!

I ALMOST FEEL SORRY FOR THIS *SKINNY FOOL.* WHILE WE HAVE THE CHILDREN, YOU WOULD NEVER *DARE* MOVE AGAINST US!

OH YEAH?

CLICK!

I DON'T BELIEVE IT, *NO POWER!*

GIVE IT HERE!

CLUNKKK!

OUR *TV REMOTE'S* ALWAYS DOING THAT!

WHIRRRRRR!

GUARDS, DON'T JUST STAND THERE. KILL THEM ALL, YOU *PITIFUL SLUMGUBBERS!*

BZZZZZT!

BZZZZZT!

AREA 26. *HOLDING PEN*. GOT TO GET *EVERYONE* OUT.

WOO-HOO!

THESE THINGS ARE *SO COOL!* WHERE DO I GET ONE?

VWOOOOOOSHH!

WE'VE *LOST THEM!*

JUST AS WELL! NOW *STAND BACK...* ANY SECOND NOW A WHOLE LOAD OF KIDS ARE GONNA COME RUNNING—

—OOUUUUUUT!

DANNY!

ABBY, YOU'RE SAFE!

NOW ALL I HAVE TO DO IS GET ABOUT *A HUNDRED-ODD THOUSAND KIDS* HOME SAFELY – AND IN TIME FOR CHRISTMAS!

HAD *WORSE DAYS,* I SUPPOSE!

MUCH LATER...

PHEW, NOW I KNOW HOW *FATHER CHRISTMAS* FEELS. I'LL NEVER CALL HIM A *MOANY OLD SLACKER* AGAIN...

MUM! DAD! YOU'LL *NEVER* GUESS WHAT...

...EVEN IF HE DOES GET *364 DAYS OFF* A YEAR!

THE END!

17

TOYBOX TERRORS!

The Eleventh Doctor once found himself trapped with scary life-sized dolls, but it wasn't the first time he'd encountered terrifying toys...

Deadly Dolls

Whenever a little boy called George got scared, he had the power to send everything he was afraid of to the dolls' house inside his cupboard. The Doctor and his friends soon found themselves trapped inside it and poor Amy got turned into a lumbering wooden doll – a state of living death! Luckily, the Doctor got George to face his fears and everyone was returned to normal in the nick of time.

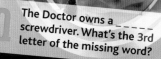

WHERE'S THE DOCTOR?

Q The Doctor owns a _ _ _ _ _ screwdriver. What's the 3rd letter of the missing word?

Ugly Troll

Thanks to the Master's meddling, this toothy troll doll was able to move about when it came into contact with heat. It tried to strangle the Third Doctor's assistant Jo Grant, but luckily it was shot to pieces before it could harm her.

Monkey Menace

The Ninth Doctor got a shock when this toy monkey suddenly started crashing its cymbals together. It was controlled by a possessed child who had the strange ability to make mechanical objects come to life.

Creepy Clowns

The evil Toymaker was a powerful being who trapped people and turned them into his playthings. Joey and Clara were two of his sinister servants. He took the two clowns from their dolls' house and watched them come eerily to life, after which they began menacing the First Doctor's companions, Steven and Dodo.

Clockwork Soldiers

The Second Doctor once found himself in the Land of Fiction where a host of made-up characters were somehow frighteningly real. He bumped into these scary clockwork soldiers who carried rifles tipped with lethal bayonets!

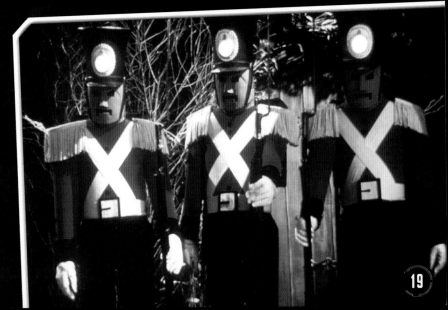

TESELECTA DATA BANK

Captain's records available for encounters between Teselecta Unit 3.2 Justice Department Vehicle and a Time Lord – designation: 'the Doctor'.

MISSING!

UPLOAD COMPLETE> 100%

MISSION: BERLIN, 1938 AD

Due to a fault in the time vector circuits, Teselecta Unit 3.2 arrived at the wrong point in Adolf Hitler's time stream. We encountered the Doctor who appeared to be dying after an assassination attempt by Melody Pond. She was on record as a criminal, but the Doctor's companions sabotaged our security systems before we could carry out full punishment.

MISSION: CALISTO B, 2437 AD

After assuming the identity of Gideon Vandaleur, Unit 3.2 investigated arms deals that were being negotiated on behalf of the Silence. The Doctor tracked us down at the docks of Calisto B and demanded information about the Silence movement. He also requested that we deliver sealed messages in blue envelopes to his most trusted allies.

RECENT TESSELATIONS

THE DOCTOR, TIME LORD

RIVER SONG/ MELODY POND

AMY POND, HUMAN

GIDEON VANDALEUR, ENVOY OF THE SILENCE

ERIC ZIMMERMAN, MEMBER OF THE NAZI PARTY

MISSION: LAKE SILENCIO, 5:02PM, 22 APRIL 2011 AD

As Captain, I authorised this special use of Teselecta Unit 3.2. While the Doctor took refuge inside our control circuits, Unit 3.2 assumed the Doctor's form, allowing him to fake his own death. I also permitted the Doctor to reprogram the exterior circuits to fake a partial Time Lord regeneration, after which Unit 3.2 was 'cremated'. As expected, minimal damage was sustained.

SPECIAL REPORT

Following the events at Utah in 2011, Unit 3.2 has attempted to track down the Doctor four times, as part of our ongoing investigations into the Silence. We have had a negative result so far, as it would appear the Doctor has disappeared...

SPOT THE DIFFERENCE

Are your powers of observation as good as the Doctor's? Find out by seeing how quickly you can spot ten differences between these two pictures.

GUESS WHO?

Gantok has fallen into a pit full of scary skulls and been eaten alive! Can you spot which four monsters have also fallen down there?

SECRETS OF
THE TARDIS

Like the Doctor, the TARDIS is the last of its kind – a triumph of Gallifreyan transdimensional engineering, even if it doesn't always work properly! And, just like its eccentric owner, there are plenty of things about it that not everyone knows...

TARDIS Type

The TARDIS is a Type 40 Mark 3 Time Travel (TT) capsule. When the Time Lords were around, they considered the Doctor's version to be completely obsolete!

Who Named It?

The name TARDIS was made up by the Doctor's granddaughter, Susan. It stands for Time And Relative Dimension In Space.

Bigger on the Inside

When the Doctor is asked how the TARDIS can possibly be bigger on the inside, he often explains that it's 'dimensionally transcendental' – whatever that means!

Who Stole Who?

The Doctor's always said he borrowed the TARDIS from his own people, but when the TARDIS matrix inhabited the body of Idris, he learned that his ship had left its doors unlocked on purpose. So, in a sense, the TARDIS stole him!

Chameleon Circuit

If the TARDIS was working properly, its Chameleon Circuit would allow it to change shape and blend in with its surroundings. However, when the First Doctor visited London, the circuit failed and the ship got stuck in the shape of a 1950s police box.

Console Copies

The TARDIS has remodelled its interior many times and the TARDIS keeps a copy of each console room for neatness. It's got about thirty so far.

TARDIS Engines

The Doctor can put his ship's engines on silent if he wants to, but says he loves the wheezing and groaning noise it normally makes.

Bits and Bobs

The Eleventh Doctor's console was rebuilt with all sorts of odds and ends, including a typewriter, a pinball machine, a gramophone trumpet — even some brass taps!

Many Rooms

No one knows how big the TARDIS really is, but over the years we've seen plenty of its rooms, including bedrooms, a cloister room, a wardrobe room, and even a swimming pool.

Instant Translator

The ship's telepathic circuits automatically translate most alien languages for the Doctor and his companions, whether spoken or written.

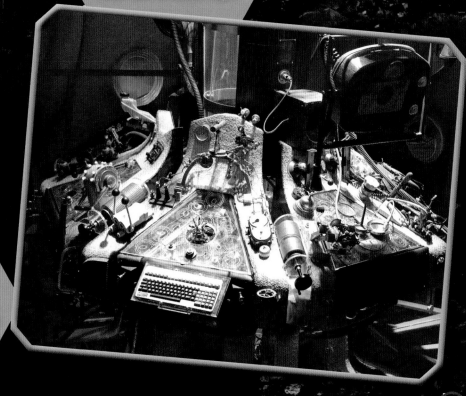

LORNA'S ESCAPE

The explosion ripped the sky apart.

Lorna Bucket looked up in time to see a spaceship engulfed in flames, thick black smoke billowing from its screaming engines as it spiralled downwards.

'Oh my God! What's that?' Lorna's friend Stefan had stopped playing in the river and was craning his neck to see above the line of trees.

Lorna shook her head in disbelief. 'Must be an accident,' she breathed, as shards of burning metal rained down onto the forest canopy below, lighting a hundred tiny fires. 'We've got to get back and tell the others!'

Then she saw it. A massive, scaly creature tumbling away from the plummeting wreck, its vast wings beating wildly as it somehow escaped the inferno. A triumphant cry burst from its massive jaws, making Lorna's heart stop. 'It's seen us!' she yelled. 'It's coming straight for us. We've got to get out of here!'

Suddenly, Lorna sensed a movement behind her and she spun round. She gasped at the sight of a tall stranger towering over her. Hand outstretched, he crouched down next to her, his wide eyes boring into hers. 'Run!'

Lorna had no idea why, but somehow she knew she could trust the stranger. She took his hand and found herself hurtling towards the shelter of the forest, her friend scrabbling after her.

Twigs and thorns tore at Lorna's bare legs as she stumbled through the undergrowth and she struggled to keep up with the stranger's lightning pace. 'Run, run, RUN!' he yelled.

'Lorna!' Stefan's scream made her glance back. Horrified, she saw that her friend had tripped and fallen over. In the same instant, the beast came crashing through the forest, its leathery wings spread wide as it came hurtling towards them.

It would be on Stefan in seconds.

'I've got to help him,' yelled Lorna. She broke free of the man's grasp and dashed back to her friend. Grabbing Stefan's arms, she quickly dragged him out of the creature's path. She glanced up – the beast's angry golden eyes burned fiercer than the blazing wreckage of the spacecraft. With a massive effort, she yanked Stefan clear, just as the monster went thundering past.

'It's OK, we're safe,' gasped Stefan, tending to his bruised leg. 'It only wanted him.'

Lorna shook her head. 'No, I think he drew it off to save us. But who is he? And what is that thing?'

Stefan shrugged. 'I don't care, I'm just glad it left us alone.'

Lorna looked at him. 'You stay here then, I'll be as quick as I can, OK?'

'Lorna, don't be stupid, you'll never–'

But Stefan's words were lost in the rustle of bushes as Lorna sped off after the creature – and the stranger. She soon heard shouts up ahead. She couldn't be certain, but it sounded like he was yelling at others, telling them to get out of the way.

Moments later, she came to a clearing and with a surge of relief she saw her father, along with a group of men from the village. 'Dad!' Lorna ran to him and threw her arms around his waist.

'Lorna, thank God! I thought we'd lost you.'

'There was a man in a green coat,' she panted. 'He must have come this way...'

'You mean the Doctor?'

Lorna frowned. 'Who's that?'

Her father led her to the edge of the clearing where the ground dropped steeply away. Lorna gasped at the scene in the hollow beyond. The creature was circling the Doctor, lashing out at him with scythe-like talons the Doctor defending himself with what looked like a small metal shield.

Lorna noticed two villagers creeping up behind the beast, their swords at the ready. But with a sudden flick of its mighty tail, the creature sent the men flailing into the air, their screams of terror cut short as their bodies slammed into the ground.

Hands clammy with sweat, Lorna watched as the Doctor tried desperately to attach a long cable to the shield, shouting and yelling as he dodged from side to side, ducking the creature's savage blows. Then suddenly, an impossibly bright light spilled out of the shield and the Doctor let out a cry of triumph. The light engulfed the snarling monster, its writhing body glowing brighter than the sun.

Then, it simply vanished.

As the villagers gasped and cheered, the stranger quickly gathered up his equipment and darted into a blue box that was half hidden in the surrounding trees. The Doctor paused in the doorway, glanced in Lorna's direction and gave the briefest of smiles. Then he slammed the door shut. With a strange grinding noise the blue box disappeared, and silence descended on the forest once more.

In the weeks that followed, life carried on much as before, but wherever she went, Lorna overheard people telling stories about the mysterious visitor and his strange wooden box.

Some claimed the Doctor must have possessed magical powers to vanquish such a terrifying beast. Others, perhaps with more imagination still, insisted the Doctor was the saviour of the Gamma Forest – that he had followed the spaceship from another world, somehow knowing that a dangerous predator would escape.

But whoever the mysterious Doctor was, one thing was clear in Lorna's mind. She knew that whatever she did, and whoever she grew up to be, one day she would have to meet the Doctor again – the mightiest warrior her world had ever known.

The Doctor's Army

When the Silence kidnapped Amy and her baby, the Doctor gathered together an unlikely band of fighters to mount a rescue. His brave friends ended up locked in a fight to the death, taking on the Headless Monks at the Battle of Demons Run...

Lorna Bucket

Lorna first met the Doctor briefly when she was a little girl. Many years later, she joined the Church's army of clerics in the hope of meeting him again, believing him to be a mighty warrior. She tried to warn the Doctor's allies that they had walked into a trap, before she was tragically killed by the Headless Monks.

Madame Vastra

The Doctor first met Madame Vastra in 19th-century London. She was venting her fury on tunnel diggers who had accidentally destroyed her colony of hibernating Silurians. Although she was a mighty warrior, Vastra would have faced certain death had the Doctor not intervened and she was only too pleased to help save Amy and her baby.

Captain Avery

Long after the Eleventh Doctor reunited him with his lost crew, Avery returned the Doctor's favour by taking over Madame Kovarian's ship, preventing her escape.

WHERE'S THE DOCTOR?

Q What is this creature called? Write down the last letter of its name.

K

Rory the Roman

Otherwise known as 'The Last Centurion', Rory cut a dash in his Roman battle gear – even though he thought he looked ridiculous! He fought bravely to defend his wife and child, little realising that the baby was really a Flesh avatar, planted by the Silence!

Commander Strax

At some point in his short twelve year life, Strax had dishonoured his fellow Sontarans. As punishment, he was ordered to nurse the weak and sick – the greatest punishment a Sontaran could be expected to endure. Also indebted to the Doctor, Strax sadly lost his life in the fight against the Headless Monks.

Jenny

On the face of it, Jenny was just a gentle, good-natured serving girl in the employ of Madame Vastra. However, when she fought alongside the Silurian warrior, she displayed breathtaking sword-fighting skills, surviving the Headless Monks' brutal attack.

The Minotaur

At first, the Doctor thought that the huge horned beast stomping through the corridors was feeding on the fears of those trapped inside the hotel. Sadly, it wasn't until people started dying that he realised the beast was actually feeding on their faith – sucking the life from its victims.

WHERE'S THE DOCTOR?

Q The Doctor's companion is called _ _ _ Pond. Write down the last letter of her first name.

welcome
To NIGHTMARE
HOTEL

The Doctor once found himself trapped inside a weird hotel where a terrifying Minotaur stalked the corridors. Scarier still, the rooms contained people's very worst fears and nightmares...

Angels of Death

The Doctor, Amy and Rory got a terrible fright when they stumbled into a room containing deadly Weeping Angels. As the lights flickered on and off, the Doctor thought the creatures would get them, but luckily, it turned out they weren't real after all!

Disturbing Dummies

A gambler called Joe found himself in a room full of the things he hated the most – dozens of grinning ventriloquists' dolls, whose wide eyes followed you as you moved around the room. When the Doctor first met him, poor Joe looked like he'd gone completely mad.

Silent Clown

When Amy and a medical student called Rita hid inside a room, they found a sinister sad-faced clown sitting on the end of the bed, staring into space!

Amy's Faith

In one room, Amy found a vision of herself as little Amelia Pond – the night she had waited for the Doctor to return for her in the TARDIS. The Doctor realised that Amy's belief in him would lead to her death, and so to save her from the Minotaur, he had to destroy her faith.

Gibbis the Coward

This timid mole-creature from Tivoli was one of the few survivors of the Minotaur's prison. His race loved to be conquered and oppressed, but the Doctor soon realised that beneath Gibbis' cowardly exterior was a sly creature with a cunning instinct for survival!

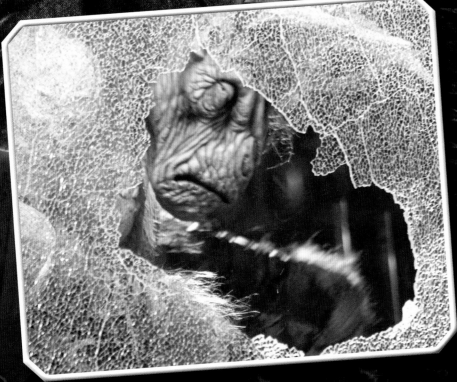

Prison In Space

The Doctor discovered that the hotel was really an automated prison in space, constructed by a race that had once worshipped the Minotaur. They had programmed the prison to trap other life forms and convert their faith into a form that would feed the creature. However, over thousands of years, the Minotaur had really only wanted to die, and thanks to the Doctor, its wish was finally granted.

THE DOCTOR'S NIGHTMARE

Even the Doctor discovered a room containing his worst fear, but no one else got to see it, except him. What do you think was in it? Was it a monster, some terror from his childhood – or something far worse? Draw it in this space!

PEG DOLL MASH-UP!

These scary Peg Dolls have somehow got all their top halves mixed up with their bottom halves. Draw a line to connect each half with its correct match.

CROSSWORD

Complete the word grid, then rearrange the letters in the red squares to finish the sentence below.

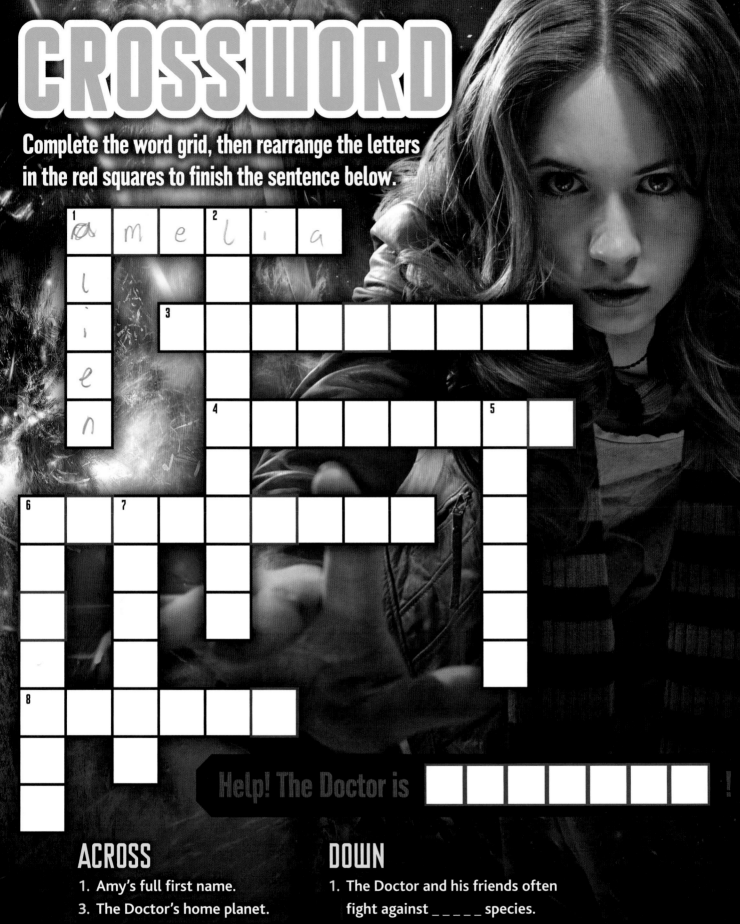

1. a m e l i a

Help! The Doctor is ⬜⬜⬜⬜⬜⬜⬜ !

ACROSS

1. Amy's full first name.
3. The Doctor's home planet.
4. Rory's last name.
6. The Doctor's wife – and Amy and Rory's daughter!
8. The number of bodies the Doctor has had so far.

DOWN

1. The Doctor and his friends often fight against _ _ _ _ _ species.
2. The village where Amy and Rory grew up.
5. The name Amy and Rory gave their baby.
6. As a child, Amy called her friend the R_ _ _ _ _ _ Doctor.
7. The TARDIS travels through the Time _ _ _ _ _ _ .

35

THE TOMB OF SHEMURA

VWORRRP!

AGGHHHH! NO, ABBY, I SAID THE *RED LEVER*. NOT THE *GREEN ONE!*

NO, NO, NO! NOW YOU'VE DE-STABILISED THE *DIMENSIONAL STABILISERS*. SWITCH THEM *ON* AGAIN!

SORRY!

PHEW! IF ANYONE'S GONNA *CRASH THE TARDIS*, IT'S GONNA BE *ME*, OK?

OK, DOCTOR!

FROM NOW ON, *YOU'RE* THE PILOT!

SUDDENLY...

SCREEEEEEECH!

WHO'S THAT?!

OWWW!

VWOOOORRRP!

WHERE'S SHE GONE?

WHOEVER IT WAS, SHE INVADED THE TARDIS'S *TELEPATHIC CIRCUITS*. A MIND THAT CAN PROJECT THAT FAR MUST BE *INCREDIBLY STRONG!*

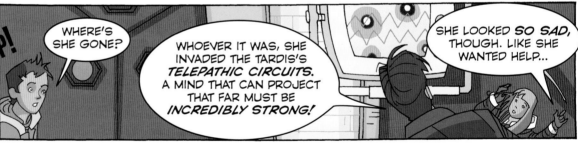

SHE LOOKED *SO SAD*, THOUGH. LIKE SHE WANTED HELP...

ACCORDING TO THIS, THE SOURCE OF THE PROJECTION IS *PHILASTRA* – PLANET OF THE *DEATHLY COLD*.

BETTER GET YOUR *WOOLLIES* ON!

SOON...

WHERE ARE ALL THE *PEOPLE?*

I DON'T KNOW. BUT SOMETHING *TERRIBLE* MUST HAVE HAPPENED HERE. I WONDER WHAT IT WAS...

SUDDENLY...

SWISHHHHHH!

FWOOOOOSH!

GET *BACK!*

PLEASE. *LET US THROUGH!*

WHAT DO YOU MEAN? HOW CAN WE *HELP YOU?*

THEY JUST *VANISHED!* WERE THEY *GHOSTS?*

NAHHH, THAT'S SILLY. MORE LIKE *AFTER-IMAGES,* RESIDUAL PSYCHIC ENERGY MANIFESTING AS *MENTAL PROJECTIONS* OF SOME KIND...

OH, OK, *GHOSTS,* IF YOU LIKE...

WHAT DO YOU THINK THEY *WANTED?*

NOT SURE... IT SEEMS THE LOCALS HAVE – OR RATHER *HAD* – ADVANCED *MENTAL POWERS.*

ANYWAY, I'VE A FUNNY FEELING WE'LL GET SOME ANSWERS IN THIS PALACE!

INSIDE...

WOW! IT'S THAT *GREEN LADY* WE SAW IN THE TARDIS. IS SHE ASLEEP?

DOESN'T LOOK LIKE SHE CAN EVEN MOVE. MAYBE IT'S A *PRISON?*

PICKING UP *FAINT LIFE SIGNS.* SHE'S IN SOME FORM OF STASIS.

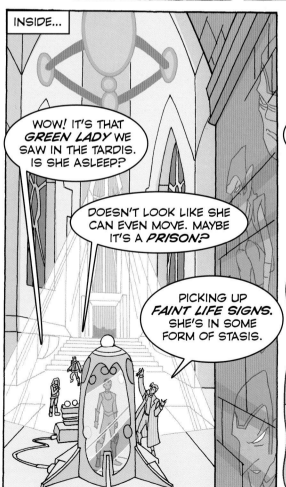

I AM *QUEEN SHEMURA.* WELCOME TO MY WORLD. I'M SORRY IF I *STARTLED YOU* EARLIER.

NOT AT ALL, NICE OF YOU TO *DROP IN!* BUT TELL ME... WHAT EXACTLY HAPPENED HERE?

I WILL SHOW YOU...

MANY YEARS AGO, THE *INVADERS* CAME. THE ATTACK WAS SWIFT. IN LESS THAN A DAY PHILASTRA WAS *IN FLAMES,* MOST OF MY SUBJECTS DEAD.

IT WAS THE *LOVE OF MY PEOPLE* THAT SAVED ME. THEY PLACED ME IN THIS CHAMBER, *PROTECTED FOREVER* FROM OUR ENEMIES.

I HOPED THAT ONE DAY THE DANGER WOULD PASS, AND *A KIND AND HANDSOME STRANGER* WOULD RELEASE ME...

HA-HA! SHE'S *GOT THE HOTS* FOR YOU, DOCTOR!

WHIRRRR

AHEM, YES... WELL... *HERE GOES!*

BUT I DON'T GET IT. HOW COME YOUR *PALACE* WASN'T DESTROYED?

FREEDOM AT LAST! YOU'RE FAR TOO SUSCEPTIBLE TO *FLATTERY*, DOCTOR.

GUARDS. *YOU ARE SUMMONED!*

HOLD ON A SECOND. WHAT'S GOING ON?

ONLY A *CRETIN* WOULD BELIEVE SUCH A *RIDICULOUS STORY.* MY SUBJECTS ROSE UP AGAINST ME. CALLED ME A *TYRANT.* THEY PAID FOR THEIR TREACHERY WITH THEIR *LIVES!*

SO RATHER THAN SURRENDER TO THE REBELLION, YOU DESTROYED YOUR OWN WORLD. *YOUR OWN PEOPLE!*

OF COURSE. NOW I HAVE YOUR *TIME VESSEL*, I CAN ESCAPE THIS *STINKING ROCK* AND CONQUER *OTHER WORLDS.* NOW, GIVE ME THE KEY TO YOUR SHIP!

NEVER! I'D RATHER DIE THAN LET A *PSYCHOPATH* LIKE YOU *LOOSE* THROUGH *SPACE AND TIME!*

YOU REALLY *ARE* A HERO, AREN'T YOU? A PITY THEY'RE ALWAYS SO *STUPID. GUARDS!*

THAT'LL DO NICELY. AND NOW, MAY YOU DIE A *HERO'S DEATH!*

CLUNKK!

WOAAAHHH!

NOOOO!

URRK!

OOF!

DANNY, YOU'RE *SQUASHING ME!*

WHAT ARE WE GONNA DO, DOCTOR? WE'RE *TRAPPED!*

OH, MY *POOR BACK...*

HOW COME THERE'S A TORCH LIT? IS SOMEONE ELSE IN HERE WITH US?

ROAAAAAARRRRR!

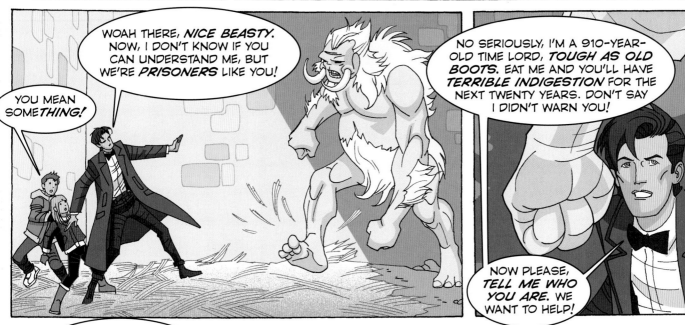

WOAH THERE, *NICE BEASTY.* NOW, I DON'T KNOW IF YOU CAN UNDERSTAND ME, BUT WE'RE *PRISONERS* LIKE YOU!

YOU MEAN SOME*THING!*

NO SERIOUSLY, I'M A 910-YEAR-OLD TIME LORD, *TOUGH AS OLD BOOTS.* EAT ME AND YOU'LL HAVE *TERRIBLE INDIGESTION* FOR THE NEXT TWENTY YEARS. DON'T SAY I DIDN'T WARN YOU!

NOW PLEASE, *TELL ME WHO YOU ARE.* WE WANT TO HELP!

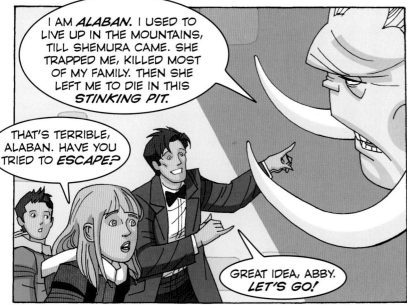

I AM *ALABAN.* I USED TO LIVE UP IN THE MOUNTAINS, TILL SHEMURA CAME. SHE TRAPPED ME, KILLED MOST OF MY FAMILY. THEN SHE LEFT ME TO DIE IN THIS *STINKING PIT.*

THAT'S TERRIBLE, ALABAN. HAVE YOU TRIED TO *ESCAPE?*

GREAT IDEA, ABBY. *LET'S GO!*

NO TIME! WE'VE GOT TO GET TO THE TARDIS BEFORE *SHEMURA* DOES!

DOCTOR, *SLOW DOWN,* WILL YOU?

BUT I'VE EXPLORED ALL THE SERVICE TUNNELS. THERE'S *NO WAY OUT!*

NO, *STOP THEM!* GUARDS!

TOO LATE! I'VE *BOOSTED THE TELEPATHIC CIRCUITS* TO FULL POWER, SHEMURA. YOU USED THEM TO BRING ME HERE...

NOW YOUR PEOPLE ARE USING THEM TO *RETURN!*

THEY'RE *IN MY HEAD.* MAKE THEM GO AWAY!

WHAT'S HAPPENING?

THE WRAITHS ARE BLOCKING SHEMURA'S *MIND CONTROL.* THE GUARDS ARE *BREAKING FREE...*

IT'S TIME YOU WENT *BACK TO SLEEP,* SHEMURA.

NO, GET OFF ME. *YOU'LL SUFFER FOR THIS!*

BACK AT THE PALACE...

STAND BACK, ALABAN! I'M GOING TO *LOCK THE CONTROLS. FOREVER!*

NOOOO!

FSSSSSSHHHH!

AMAZING, THAT'S SORTED HER OUT!

WELL DONE, ALABAN. WILL YOU BE OK?

I'LL BE FINE, DOCTOR. I'LL GO BACK TO THE MOUNTAINS, MAYBE SOME OF MY FAMILY SURVIVED.

ACTUALLY, THAT REMINDS ME...

WHAT?

YOUR MUM AND DAD MUST BE WONDERING WHERE *YOU TWO* ARE!

I TOLD THEM WE'D ONLY BE *FIVE MINUTES!*

THE END!

THE CYBER FILES

One of the Doctor's greatest enemies, the Cybermen have one single purpose – to convert other life forms into cold, unfeeling beings like themselves.

Genesis of the Cybermen

The Cybermen originated from Earth's twin planet Mondas. Once human like us, the people of Mondas gradually replaced parts of their bodies with plastic and metal. They considered emotions to be a weakness and so removed them from their brains.

Cyber Variants

On a parallel world, the Cybermen were created by businessman John Lumic as a way of extending human life. His grisly 'upgrading' process involved removing a person's brain and placing it inside a metal exoskeleton!

Rory's Face-off

When the Silence kidnapped Amy, Rory bravely infiltrated the command centre of the Twelfth Cyber Legion to find out where his wife had been taken. Meanwhile, the Doctor took the opportunity to blow up dozens of Cyber ships!

Cybermen in Colchester

While visiting his friend Craig, the Doctor discovered a group of Cybermen whose ship had crash-landed centuries before. The once-dormant cyborgs had started tapping into nearby power lines and were busy converting others into emotionless Cybermen!

Controller Craig

The Cybermen tried to turn poor Craig into their Controller by encasing his head in a metal helmet and removing his emotions. However, when Craig heard his baby crying, the sudden influx of emotions overloaded the Cybermen's emotional inhibitors and they all exploded!

Sneaky Cybermat

This tiny metal rat-creature was used by the Cybermen to drain electrical energy from the surrounding area. Beneath its smooth metal casing was a set of lethal, razor-sharp fangs!

The Eleventh Doctor
Super-Quiz

1
Who's just shot the TARDIS console?
a) Canton
b) Mels
c) A Cyberman

2
On which planet did the Doctor encounter the Weeping Angels?
a) Phijax 4
b) Alfava Metraxix
c) Apalapucia

3
What message did George send the Doctor?
a) Please save me from the monsters!
b) The monsters want to eat me!
c) Look out, the monsters are coming!

WHERE'S THE DOCTOR?

Q **What's this monster called?** Write down the 4th letter of its name in the space.

4

The Doctor met living copies of real people. What were they known as?
a) Dupoids
b) Carbon-Clones
c) Gangers

5

Where did the Doctor meet creatures from Saturnyne?
a) Rome
b) Venice
c) Paris

6

What's about to happen to Purcell?
a) He gets turned to stone.
b) He turns into a big pool of gooey slime.
c) He gets turned into a doll.

7

The Doctor met this man on an alien planet. What is his name?
a) Zoltan Vadis
b) Kazran Sardick
c) Talran Marvic

8 What was the name of this cube-shaped prison box?
a) Pandora's Box
b) The Pandorica
c) The Prison of Rassilon

9 Which alien creature did the Eleventh Doctor first encounter?
a) An Eknodine
b) Prisoner Zero
c) A Krafayis

10 Professor Bracewell believed he had created the Daleks – but what did he call them?
a) Ironsides
b) Metaltrons
c) Megatanks

11 These reptilian warriors helped the Doctor at a great battle. Where did it take place?
a) Demons World
b) Demons Star
c) Demons Run

12 How long did Amy wait for the Doctor and Rory on Apalapucia?
a) Sixteen years
b) Twenty-six years
c) Thirty-six years

13 What was so interesting about Gibbis's home planet, Tivoli?
a) It had twenty-three suns.
b) It was the most invaded planet in the galaxy.
c) No one could ever find it!

14 Which evil entity took control of this Ood?
a) House
b) The Dream Lord
c) The Mara

15 Before meeting his fate at Lake Silencio, which old friend did the Doctor visit?
a) Craig Owens
b) Craig Jones
c) Craig Holmes

ESCAPE THE MINOTAUR!

Find a way through the maze back to the TARDIS before the Minotaur feeds on your faith and reduces you to a brainless zombie!

START

FINISH

POLICE PUBLIC CALL BOX

SHADOW MATCH

The Doctor's lurking in the shadows... Test your observation skills and see if you can work out which of the two silhouettes below match exactly.

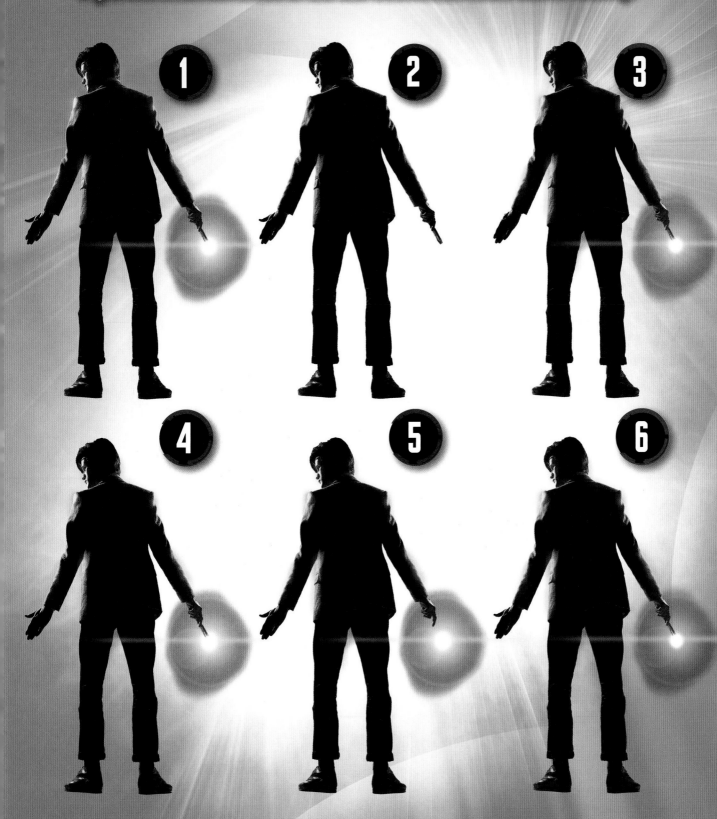

THE LIFE AND TIMES OF RIVER SONG

It's tricky keeping up with River Song and the Doctor since they're forever meeting in the wrong order. To help, here's a handy time traveller's guide to River's greatest adventures – but watch out for spoilers...

Born in Battle

After Amy is taken prisoner by the Silence, she gives birth on an asteroid called Demons Run. Amy names her precious daughter Melody Pond.

Melody Kidnapped

The Silence abduct Melody and take her to Earth. They raise her with one purpose in life – to kill the Doctor – but she manages to escape. Living rough on the streets of New York, she ends up regenerating into a new body.

First Meeting

After making her way to England, Melody becomes the best friend of young Amy and Rory and grows up alongside her parents! Known as Mels, she eventually meets the Doctor – and almost wrecks his TARDIS!

Kill the Doctor!

In 1930s Berlin, Mels is shot by Adolf Hitler and regenerates into the body that will become known as River Song. River carries out her programming and kills the Doctor, but Amy and Rory convince her to save him and she does so by sacrificing her remaining lives.

Trapped in a Spacesuit

River studies archaeology and eventually becomes a doctor herself. But the Silence haven't finished with her yet... They kidnap her yet again, force her into an Apollo spacesuit, and place her under Lake Silencio in Utah.

Time Collapses

Although the Doctor's death at Lake Silencio is a fixed point, River refuses to kill him and so all of time begins to unravel. In an alternative reality, the Doctor marries her and she learns that he cheated death by hiding inside his Teselecta duplicate!

Identity Revealed

River ends up in prison for killing the Doctor, but she later breaks out and appears at Demons Run, not long after the Silence kidnapped her baby self. She tells a shocked Amy and Rory who she really is – their grown-up daughter, Melody!

Prison Break

After receiving an invitation from the Doctor, River breaks out of prison again. She joins Amy and Rory at Lake Silencio, and watches her younger self shooting down the Teselecta Doctor. However, she has to pretend she doesn't know what's really happening!

The Pandorica Opens

Breaking out of prison again, River joins the Doctor as he investigates the mysterious Pandorica. She becomes trapped at the centre of his exploding TARDIS, but he saves her and she helps him in his plan to reboot the universe!

War with Angels

River teams up with the Doctor on the planet Alfava Metraxis where they battle against the Weeping Angels. Before going back to prison, River admits to the Doctor that she killed the best man she ever knew...

River's rivals

Check out some of the aliens and adversaries that River Song's fought against!

The Vashta Nerada

The Daleks

The Weeping Angels

The Silence

Visiting Amy

Immediately after her fight against the Weeping Angels, River sneaks a visit to her mother on Earth. Amy still thinks that the Doctor was killed at Lake Silencio, but River reveals the incredible news that he's still alive!

Last Goodbye

The Doctor, in his tenth incarnation, meets River for the first time. She stops him from sacrificing himself to save the people trapped inside the Library, and gives up her own life instead. However, the Doctor manages to preserve her consciousness in the Library's computer, where she carries on living a virtual life.

FOREST OF FEAR

In a sentient forest on another world, the Doctor and his new friends met a creepy King and Queen made out of wood...

Following Footprints

After sneaking through a space-time portal disguised as a Christmas present, Cyril Arwell found himself in a magical alien forest. He followed strange footprints in the snow that kept on getting bigger and bigger as they went along!

WHERE'S THE DOCTOR?

The Doctor met Cyril _ _ _ _ _ _ one Christmas. What's the 3rd letter of Cyril's surname?

Tower of Trees

At last, Cyril came to a tall building which wasn't really a building at all. It was actually a bunch of intelligent trees that had somehow disguised themselves in the shape of a stone tower. The Doctor and

The King and Queen

Inside the tower, two weird wooden figures were waiting for Cyril — the King and Queen of the forest. When the Queen trapped him and placed a glowing crown on his head, Cyril could suddenly hear the whole forest screaming. The poor trees were all terrified of something…

Soul Saver

The Doctor discovered that the forest was about to be destroyed with acid rain, and that the trees needed to use a living thing to help their souls escape. The only person that could help them was Cyril's mum, Madge. She carried the trees' life force inside her head so they could begin a new life among the stars!

ESCAPE FROM THE SILENCE!

Play this game with your friends – and see who'll be the first to reach the TARDIS alive!

START

13 Stop to record sightings of your enemy. Miss a turn!

12

14

11

15

10

16

1

2 You discover the Silents' underground spaceship. Run forward 4 spaces!

9 You resist interrogation. Throw again!

17

3

18

8

7

19

4

5 You bump into a Silent, but forget you've seen it. Go back to the start!

6

20 The Doctor implants a nanorecorder into your palm. Sneak forward 4 spaces.

21

22

HOW TO PLAY

1 Use one counter (such as a coin or button) for each player.

2 Take turns to roll a die and move your counter round the board.

3 When you land on a space with an instruction on it, you must do what it says.

4 The winner is the first person to reach the TARDIS, but you have to throw the right number to win!

32

33

Take off your eye-drive before the Silence get you! Go forward 2 spaces.

34

31

35

Ambushed by the Silence! Go back to number 15.

30

36

29

37

28

You're completely surrounded by the Silence, go back 6 spaces.

27

38

39 Marry River Song. Throw a 2 to win!

26

POLICE PUBLIC CALL BOX

POLICE PUBLIC CALL BOX

The Silence trap you inside a spacesuit. Throw a 6 to break out!

25

40

24

23

FINISH
WELL DONE!

PUZZLE ANSWERS

Page 22 Spot the Difference

Page 23 Guess Who?
1) Dalek; 2) Silurian; 3) Weeping Angel;
4) Minotaur

Page 34 Peg Doll Mash-Up!
A)3; B)5; C)4; D)2; E)1

Page 35 Crossword

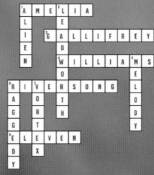

The Doctor is missing

Page 44-47 Eleventh Doctor

Super-Quiz
1)b; 2)b; 3)a; 4)c; 5)b; 6)c; 7)b; 8)b; 9)b;
10)a; 11)c; 12)c; 13)b; 14)a; 15)a

p48 Escape the Minotaur!

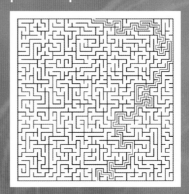

Page 49 Shadow Match
Shadows 1 and 6 match exactly.

WHERE'S THE DOCTOR?

Did you solve the picture clues and find all the letters? Re-arrange them in the spaces below to spell the name of the Doctor's destination!

DOCTOR WHO
THE OFFICIAL
DOCTIONARY

Doctionary *(essential book)* the Doctor's dictionary of definitions for time travellers

COMING SOON!

Page 59 Where's the Doctor? The Doctor's destination is New York.

59

DORIUM'S PROPHECY

While searching for information about the mysterious Silence, the Doctor gets a rather disturbing glimpse of his own future...

Beheaded in Battle

At the Battle of Demons Run, Dorium Maldovar tries to sweet talk the Headless Monks out of killing him, knowing that they are old customers of his. Unfortunately for him, the Monks have other ideas and they swiftly decapitate him, storing his living head inside a wooden box!

The First Question

The Doctor manages to track down Dorium, keen to know why the Silence want him dead. Dorium's information isn't very reassuring... According to him, the Silence want to avert the Doctor's future at all costs, and are determined that he must never reach the Fields of Trenzalore. They believe that in that very place, the oldest question in the universe will be asked. A question that the Doctor has been running from all his life...

DID YOU KNOW?

The Doctor once told River Song his real name, but most people still don't know what it is!

On the Fields of Trenzalore

At the Fall of the Eleventh

When no living creature can speak

Falsely or fail to answer

A question will be asked

A question that must never

ever be answered...

DOCTOR WHO?